The Blood is Compulsory

Nick Tarras

Table of Contents

Content Warning

This book contains sexual content. It is not intended for anyone under the age of adulthood. All characters depicted in sexual situations herein are over 18 of age. This book is not to be used as an informational guide to any type of sex or sexual education.

Some content within this book may be triggering or disturbing to some readers. Reader discretion is advised.

This book features: **Ritualistic self-harm, blood play.**

I

The doors to Lamuker's temple are twice as tall as the average human.

It's an exercise in patience, you've been told. If one were to rush their way through, the doors would snap behind them in an indescriptible racket. To avoid the judgmental eyes of other followers, there is no other choice but to shut the door manually and carefully, so that it will close without a sound. The very act of going to the temple, prior to even praying, is thus supposed to make one more virtuous.

Naturally, you barge in by kicking the door open.

"Simin!" You call. If your voice weren't loud enough already, the echo of the door slamming shut certainly announced your presence. The blaring noise is *immensely* satisfying.

You hear the familiar claps of footsteps; one, two, three- and there she is, Simin, her golden robes reflecting the sunlight like dragon scales. She's a beautiful woman, this priestess; tall, curly hair falling right below her ears, her skin a rich brown like fertile earth after a heavy rain. She would be very attractive, were she not one of the most irritating people you've ever been given the displeasure to meet.

"Aurum." She shoots back a smile that is really just teeth. "I would love to say that you are welcome here, but lies are frowned upon in this holy place."

"The feeling is mutual, believe me." You stride towards her. "But due to unforeseen events, I have to ask for your… cooperation."

She raises an eyebrow at that. Her robes adorn absurdly long sleeves, which you're certain she must be using as extra pockets. She tucks her hands in them as you get closer. "You came to ask *me*. For a *favor?*"

"It's not a *favor*." You quickly correct her. You would rather die than be indebted to her. "It's a problem that will affect the both of us unless we manage to work together, much as I loathe the thought. See, one of my people wishes to marry one of yours."

Her eyes widen in surprise. Evidently, that is not how she expected your sentence to end. "Who?"

"Rosae, the florist by the lakeside." A good girl. She brings flowers to the temple of Dum every once in a while. It smells better than incense. "And the runemaker by the market."

"Leila?" Simin takes her hands out of her sleeves to massage her temples. "I refuse. I will not marry these girls."

"What do you mean you *refuse?!*" Anger rises in your throat, sharp and cold like shards of ice rolling off your tongue. "You cannot refuse. We are *priests*. If they wish to be married, it is our *duty* to get them so. You can't just refuse on the grounds that you don't like us."

"Do you truly think I'm that petty?" Yes. Absolutely. One hundred percent. "I'm not refusing out of personal dislike. I'm refusing because you people are everything Lamuker stands against. There is no way she would approve of the union between one of her followers and one of Dum's."

She glances to the side saying that, to the effigy of Lamuker. The serpentine statue towers over the both of you, wings spread, fangs bared in what could either be a welcoming smile or a threatening snarl.

You care not for that statue. She is not your god. She's not even a god at all, as far as you're concerned. You have no reason to be intimidated by it.

"You asked her directly? In the past ten seconds I've been talking to you? Why, Simin, with such talent, you should not be a priestess, but a carrier pigeon!" You take a step forward. She's slightly taller than you, but this has never stopped you from picking fights with her (sometimes *very* literally.) "Is it not heresy to use your god's name to spread your own agenda?"

Her hand darts forward to grab a fistful of your collar. "Do not presume to know more about my god than I do, *Aurum*." She hisses, a perfect mirror of the reptile she worships.

You hold her gaze, unmoving. You both know her hands are tied. She cannot risk a fight here. You might spill blood on holy ground.

Eventually, she lets go of you, and starts pacing in circles. "What about you? You who call us *khaesaes*. Wouldn't your god object to such a union?"

Khaesaes. From the Sand Tongue, *khaesan*, false gods, and the suffix *-ae*, people of, those related to. *Khaesaes*. Worshippers of false gods.

"Dum does not care." You answer bluntly. "His opinion takes precedence over mine. Though if you're so interested in my personal thoughts on this- while I find your belief system confusing, I hold nothing against khaesaes. If you guys want to send your prayers to overglorified mages, be my guest. I only dislike you, personally, on an individual level."

"You truly know how to speak to women." She replies curtly. Though, when she speaks again, her voice holds slightly less vitriol than usual. "You should leave, Aurum. There is no way this can work, and you know why."

You do know why. You had said the same thing to the florist girl, at the time. But she had looked at you with those pleading eyes, and you had thought you owed her at least an *attempt.*

At least, when these girls will come back to you to ask how it went, you'll be able to say with complete honesty that *you* had tried your best.

II

Dum's temple is a small thing nestled between a hattery and a potion brewery. It can comfortably fit about a dozen people (and twice as much if one ditches the comfort part.) It's sparse in furniture as well: an altar, a couple chairs, a shelf for scriptures.

It's been built this way, first and foremost, for practicality reasons: Sand People are a minority in this town. So long as they don't all decide to come pray on the exact same day, this much space is more than enough. Additionally, the temple is far from overflowing with donations, so you did not get ambitious when designing its plans.

The temple itself doesn't matter, either way. It could be a shack, a tent, or even the naked sky for all Dum cares. The only, the one primordial piece, is the altar.

The stone table feels cold under your elbows. Your hands are joined under your chin, your eyes closed. Blood drips down your slit wrists.

You are praying.

Vaguely, you hear the door cracking open, and you open an eyelid. You recognize Simin's tall form, bending over to go through the door. The sight makes you smile. Soon enough though, you close your eyes again.

You hear her step closer, then stop. You do not speak. Neither does she. Incompatible as the two of you may be, the both of you are still priests. As a servant to the divine from another, you know one does not interrupt a prayer.

After a while, you open your eyes again. You reach out for the knife laid on the altar. The silver blade is carved with runes. You press the flat of it against your wrist, and you feel a familiar tickle as the wound closes.

Only then, do you finally spare a glance at Simin. Her gaze has zeroed on your arms, on the red still painting your skin. Predictably, her face is distorted into a scowl, repulsion emanating from her every pore.

Of course. Of course. To Lamuker, there is no greater taboo than to spill blood. To Dum, it is a necessary offering for any prayer.

The two of you truly are incompatible.

"Can I help you, Simin?" You ask, voice as sickeningly sweet as you can manage. You then reach for the rag you keep below your altar to wipe your wrists clean. Your own priest garb is sleeveless; you might stain the silver cloth otherwise.

Your voice seems to break her out of her trance. Her gaze suddenly snaps back to your face. Her teeth are grit, and when you glance down, you can see that her fists are clenched. Her disgust fills you with pride. "You know damn well why I am here, Aurum."

"Oh, please. As if *you* didn't get a kick out of me asking you for a favor last time." You put the rag away, then turn to go grab a chair. "What changed your mind?"

"..." You don't get to see her expression at that moment. As she is silent, you can't go off her tone of voice either. Unfortunate. "It's that florist girl. She was so… hopeful. I couldn't break that joy."

Ah. Well.

Much as you hate Simin, you do have to say you relate on this one.

"So," you turn back and set the chair next to her. "What's the plan?"

She does not sit down. "I suppose we could start by comparing attires," she grumbles, "that's as good a place to start as any."

"Simin." That attempt was honorable, but you will not be complicit to her ignoring the problem. "Dum needs blood for a marriage to be officialized. From the both of them."

The golden-clad woman sighs. "Of *course* you degenerates would necessitate blood on a day meant to be joyful."

Your eye twitches, but you do not take the bait. "Obviously." You step closer to her. She refuses to back away, meaning the two of you end up almost chest to chest. You have to crane your neck to keep looking at her in the eyes. "What gift is more precious, more personal than your own blood? How could you even *consider* giving anything else to your beloved?"

She rolls her eyes. "Warp it in as many pretty words as you want. It's still pain. It's still hurt."

"It doesn't have to be. We have tools for that purpose." You nod towards the knife behind her. "Dum is a god of blood, not pain. It can be painless, then healed up right afterwards."

Simin groans. You can visibly see her struggle not to protest. You're impressed. She seems to *genuinely* be trying to compromise. "I suppose," and you can tell those words cost her, "that you could always make her bleed. If that's *truly* necessary."

Wait. What?

"No, I can't do it." You clarify quickly. "They have to be the ones doing it. They have to make each other bleed. *They're* the ones who wish to get married."

"... *What?!*" Her voice is suddenly freezing like ice. "No. Absolutely *not*. This is the one, the *one* rule we cannot compromise with. *The one!*" Her hand darts forward and she suddenly grabs your shoulder. "*You shall not spill blood.* The *one* fucking rule, and you know it, Aurum!"

"Oh, so *we* should be the ones to make all the compromises, huh?" You slap her hand away. "You're not so important that I am making these rules specifically to fuck with *you,* Simin. There are reasons and symbols behind these."

You slam your own hands on her shoulders, pushing her backward. She stumbles until the back of her thighs hit the edge of the stone table. You press on, drawing as uncomfortably close as you can. This temple is *your* territory, and you will not let some Sea Folk who worships *a damn snake* tell you to bow down and abandon the *one* cornerstone of your worship.

"Listen here, *Simin,*" you bare your teeth as you speak, leaning forward to truly corner her, "no blood, *no wedding.* End of discussion. So *you* go and dig through your thousand nonsensical legends to see if you can find some loophole to-"

Your knee finds something hard, and warm, Simin suddenly *inhales,* and you forget the rest of your sentence.

Slowly, your gaze trails down.

Oh.

Oh.

"Don't- don't flatter yourself," Simin seethes, equally mortified and venomous. She's not looking at you. "It's just been a while. You're not *that* attractive."

"What, does your goddess also forbid you from the pleasures of the flesh?"

"Of *course* not. What kind of stupid rule would that be?" A pause. And then, through grit teeth: "but it *is* a sin to use your position to gain favors. You can understand that much, can't you?"

Ah… yes. It physically hurts you to do so, but you must admit that this rule, for once, makes sense. That is not a problem you ever had to deal with; priests simply aren't that influential in your culture. But False Gods are always made to be so powerful, so all-compassing, so omnipotent. Their priests are much more respected. It must be hard to know whether fellow worshippers would agree to anything out of free will or out of obligation.

You do some quick math in your head. It's been a while for you too; sex is not something you have ever felt an active hunger towards. That being said, it is still an activity you find pleasurable. It doesn't hurt that Simin, for all your mutual beef, is quite easy on the eye.

"Would you like some help with that, then?"

Simin whips her head towards your face. Her eyes are wide, scrutinizing you with an intensity you have come to associate with her being about to call you out on your bullshit. Her sudden and undivided attention sends a shiver down your spine. "What?"

"We are both priests. We are of equal standing. I am not even of your faith. You cannot take advantage of me. What I offer is not for any sort of gain, nor for fear of any retribution. So, I am asking you," you press your knee against her, and she *gasps,* pure honey to your ears, "would you like some help with *that?"*

For a second, she does nothing; she does not kiss you, nor does she shove you away. She stares, and you know what she's thinking; you know she's trying to determine how serious you are about this.

"Say the word, Simin, and I will never bring this up again." You grin. "Or will bring it up at a later date, if that's what you would prefer."

She snorts at that; and though the tension does not completely leave her shoulders, you can tell most of her wariness does. "Suck my dick, Aurum."

It's an insult, it's a taunt, it's a challenge, and, most importantly, it's a *yes*.

You shove her again, and she reaches up to grab your shoulders, sending you both tumbling on top of the altar. Your mouths meet in a crash. She doesn't bite, surprisingly enough, but that doesn't make that kiss in any way *gentle*. She's fierce, as if this too were a fight, and it's that attitude more than the physical sensations that truly gets to you. Her hands move to your hips, holding you so firmly you *know* you will bruise.

Finally, the two of you break apart, panting. You set your palms on each side of her head and push yourself up, hovering above her.

You have read, a long time ago, that the word *sacrifice* comes from the old Sea Tongue: *sacer,* sacred, and *facere,* to make, to do. *Sacrifice.* To make something holy.

Simin certainly looks the part, here, hair sprayed around her head, chest fluttering up and down. There is something almost divine, in her shortened breaths, in the heat of her skin.

Your eyes flicker towards her arms. There are red spots, staining her golden sleeves. Blood. Your blood, which you had spilled earlier. Your blood, which you have pushed her on. *Your* blood, corrupting the robes of Lamuker's priest, yours, yours, *you* did this to her.

"Do you plan on actually *doing* anything, or should I go ahead and take care of myself?"

You chuckle. "Isn't patience a virtue to your people, Simin?" But you sit back on your heels, one leg on each side of her hips, and reach out to undo her sash. You part her robes, letting your hands linger over the smooth skin of her stomach. "Though seeing you pleasing yourself is *definitely* something I would love to see another time."

You kiss her Adam's apple, feeling it bob beneath your lips. Then you trail lower; her sharp collarbone, her firm breasts, her taut stomach. You slide your way off the altar, dragging her underwear over her deliciously muscular thighs.

"You people kneel to pray, do you not?"

She tilts her head up to raise an eyebrow at you, as if to say, *what of it?*

Good. All the better to see you drop on your knees.

She gasps as you kiss her inner thigh, her face at the crossroad between astonishment, reverence, and pleasure. *"Goddess."*

You chuckle at that. "No. Not in this place, she isn't." And you lick a long stripe on the side of her cock.

The noise she makes is *heavenly.* Her hands come up to grab onto your shoulders. You can feel her fingers tremble above your robe.

You want to drive her insane. You want to make her forget that she might draw blood. You want to see what it takes to turn these trembling hands into a grip that will *bruise.*

You lick her again, methodically, mapping every inch of her length as you hunt for her most pleasurable spots. One of her hands leaves you to cover her mouth. Suits herself. That only makes the moans that do escape her all the sweeter.

She likes it best, you find, when you tease the underside of her head. Kissing her thighs earns you a delicate hum. Kissing her base has her tugging at you to go back up. She's so warm, beneath your lips, warm and hard and *heavy.* She's not on the long side of things; but she *does* have a sizable girth. It makes you wonder how she'd feel like in your mouth. So you part your lips, and take her in.

The hand still on your shoulder *squeezes,* so hard it hurts, and you think *ah, there we go.*

"*Aurum,*" she calls. *Aurum,* in the same tone she'd said *goddess. Aurum,* a whisper, a whimper, a prayer. Your gaze flutters upward, to be greeted by a wonderful sight; Simin, prompted on her elbow, chest heaving rapidly, *devouring* you with her eyes.

You would smirk, were your mouth not already full. Instead, your cast your eyes back down and bob your head.

24

She comes a few minutes later, undone by the swirl of your tongue and the pressure of your lips. You make a show to swallow it all. It tastes bitter, but the look on her face is well worth it.

The next few minutes pass in silence. You clean yourself up as she catches her breath. Your shoulder aches when you adjust your robes. She might have actually left a mark, with how tightly she held onto you. That thought fills you with pride. You will have to check tomorrow morning.

"You..." Simin finally speaks up, "if the temple is ever in need of money, you should consider working in a brothel."

"Do my ears deceived me? Simin, is that a *compliment?*"

She rolls her eyes in response. "Don't get ahead of yourself. You're still an unsufferable bastard and I pray every day for a weasel to find its way in your pantry. But I do have to admit… that your skills are… alright."

It clearly physically pains her to say so. You burst out in laughter, and she glares daggers at you in response. "Why, thank you! I will keep that in mind should I need to reconsider my career."

(You very much won't. Your body is, unfortunately, unfit for any kind of sex work. Flattery is flattery though, and any you can get out of Simin is one you deeply appreciate.)

"Also," you chuck a spare robe at her. She catches it, eyebrows knit in confusion. "You should change. You're still covered in me."

"… *I'm sorry?*" She quickly glances down, looking for any trace of your come on her legs. Oh, Simin. Messing with her is the pinnacle of comedy.

"Wrong fluids, Simin." You point at your own back. "Behind you."

She twists around. You see the exact moment her eyes catch sight of the blood on her garb. The lips curl into a snarl, disgust and anger both flashing through her eyes. "Mother*fucker!*"

III

Simin does not come back by the temple.

That was expected, honestly. Going to her now would only make her even more of a bitch to deal with, so you dutifully do your part and avoid her temple as well. For the next few days, you pray, guide followers, buy groceries, and generally live your life as if nothing had happened. The two of you briefly run into each other by the market, which is on your top ten most awkward moments in your life, but she takes a sharp turn to the left and you do not follow her.

It's five days in that you find the letter on your doorstep, set neatly on folded set of your robes.

It doesn't say anything substantial. Just a date, an hour, and an address. It's not even signed.

You understand. Simin wants to meet on neutral territory. Not her temple, not yours; somewhere unrelated to you both.

That is fine by you. You do find it funny that you managed to suck her off so good she fears to lose her footing if she steps in your lane again, but you have to appreciate that she isn't trying to drag you in a place where the very walls loathe your faith. The two of you have to find a way to work together *somehow,* so you won't spit into an offered palm.

So you follow her instructions and meet her at her chosen date, in a small restaurant by the port.

"You know," you say, blowing on your soup, "I genuinely thought you guys couldn't eat meat."

She quirks an eyebrow up, pausing her knife. "…Why? That would be one weirdly specific taboo."

"Your faith is made of *nothing* but weirdly specific taboos. Food rules wouldn't be that out of place." You point out. "Mostly though, I meant that it's hard to obtain meat without making a living creature bleed."

Simin rolls her eyes. "Hard is not the same thing as impossible. If a blade is hot enough, the flesh cauterizes as you cut it, and you can slice the meat without a single drop of blood." Huh, really? You'd never thought of that before. You figure it's a similar magic to the one carved in your prayer knife. Not something you thought you'd have in common with Lamuker's cult, not gonna lie.

"Usually though, butchers and doctors have special permission to shed blood. These are hereditary jobs among Sea Folks." She continues, briefly pausing to bite on her food. "This isn't as necessary as it used to, though. Ever since our borders opened, plenty of people of different faiths have come in, and they're more than willing to do these jobs for us."

Huh, that is actually quite interesting. "What about soldiers? Does the temple grant them bleeding privileges?"

Simin shakes her head. "No. If we need to defend ourselves, fire is our go-to."

Oh! That explains a lot. "So *that's* why your cuisine is like that. It's all about boiling and roasting and frying here. It tastes good, don't get me wrong, but it was surprising to see when I first came here."

Now she's the one to look intrigued. "Do Sand People cook differently?"

"We do. Usually we cook things on heated stones, or by burying them in hot sand. It's a low-heat, long-time cooking process."

She nods through your explanation. "I didn't take you for a chief."

"I like cooking." You say simply. That, and also you've yet to find a restaurant that serves dishes from back home, so you have to do it yourself. Again, you like Sea Folk cuisine just fine, but… a guy gets nostalgic at times, you know? "What of you? Got any hobby aside from being a pain in my ass?"

"Oh, but pissing you off is *so* satisfying." She kicks you under the table. "I like to paint, if you must know. Don't expect to see anything of mine though. I burn the completed pieces."

"Too ugly for this world?"

"Not as ugly as your face."

You snort. What a weak insult. She's losing her bite, truly. "I sense a pattern with the fire, though. Is this something we need to include in the marriage?"

"It's not *necessary*." She says. "It would be a nice touch, though," and just like that, the discussion goes back to business.

IV

You walk away from that meeting with an outline of a plan concerning logistics, a good idea of what clothes to prepare, and some dishes to look up, which is progress. You, however, still have no idea how to solve the blood problem.

That is inconvenient.

Two days later, you decide to go see Simin at her temple. You doubt you could convince her to set foot in Dum's residence again, and this is the kind of matter you cannot discuss in public, since the two of you will surely get heated as always. (Heated as in throwing hands. Not as in sex. Though you wouldn't mind *this* kind of heated becoming the norm.)

You come in late, so as to not disturb any regular follower of Lamuker. You barge in just as loudly as the last time, slamming the doors behind you. Surprisingly though, there is no sight of Simin this time; the temple is empty, save for the effigy of its goddess.

You walk up to the statue. Dum does not have a physical form. No god does; and that is but one of the many differences between deities and khaesans. That is why, as you are not currently arguing with Simin, you can't help but feel fascinated by Lamuker's image.

The carver did an amazing work, you have to admit. Each scale of the snake has been lovingly rendered, from the tip of her tail to the edge of her snout. Her face, too, is quite incredible up close. Bared fangs and unhinged jaws, threat and smile all at once.

Your pondering is interrupted by footsteps. "Aurum? It's you, isn't it? Would it kill you to be gentler with this door? One day you *will* bring down the whole temple with it."

You turn around to face her. "Oh, please. With how thick these columns are, it'd take more than that to-"

Your eyes widen.

Red. Red on Simin's fingers, red on her palms, red on her wrists. She's holding her hands on top of one another to stop the blood from dripping on the floor. Shining, bright red, all over her skin , and you *know* blood that is too much to be walking around too much not to be *dangerous.*

"Did you get hurt?!" Alarm rises in your throat. You rush towards her, your gaze already trying to locate the source of the bleeding-

Simin raises both hands in the air, palms facing you. "I'm fine. It's paint."

Oh.

Oh.

You- of course it's paint. You *know* blood. This didn't smell as much. Besides- you know *Simin.* If *nothing else,* the prospect of dropping blood onto sacred ground would have made her react more strongly than this.

She laughs at your face. "What, were you *worried* about me, Aurum?"

"Yeah, it's called common human decency, dunno if you've heard of it." You spit back. She… well, she scared you here. "I want you to fall down the stairs, not to *die,* you braindead idiot."

She has the galls to sound *surprised* at your response, the absolute asshole. Does she think this lowly of you? This actually kind of hurt, not gonna lie.

"… *Anyways,*" and just like that, the topic of how much and how little you care about her is closed, "I need to wash my hands. We can talk afterwards."

You make a vague gesture of the hand. "Go right ahead, I'll be waiting. You look like me after a prayer like this."

You mean that as a joke, yet Simin's shoulders visibly tense up. "I am aware," she says, and hurries out of the room.

… Huh.

Huh.

Well that was. Weird.

You remember your conversation the other day. *I like to paint, if you must know. Don't expect to see anything of mine though. I burn the completed pieces.* She never did elaborate as to why she destroyed her paintings afterwards.

You shake your head. This is probably unrelated. Knowing Simin, she must simply dislike being compared to the height of heresy.

You sit on a bench until she finally comes back, her hands tucked safely within her sleeves. "So."

"So."

She leans against the altar, a tall wooden table adorned with unlit candles, and you speak up. "You know what I want to talk about."

To your surprise, she does not immediately deny it, nor does she advocate for her no-blood rule. Instead, she stays silent for a few seconds, staring at you, until finally: "Why the blood?"

You blink. "Come again?"

"The last time we talked about it. Before we got… distracted. You told me there were rules and symbolisms and whatnot. Tell me about these. Why is the blood compulsory?"

Oh.

She's never asked before.

"It's about…" You trail off, trying to find the best way to word it. "Half of it is about the intimacy. As I told you; there is nothing more precious, more personal, than your own blood. It's your *life,* made liquid. It's something that belongs to you and no one else. To offer it to your partner is the greatest mark of affection."

You get up and take hold of your arm. She raises an eyebrow at you, but seeing that she makes no move to take her arm away, you gently pull her hand out of her sleeve. Then, you flip it palm up. You notice they're still humid from their earlier washing.

"The other part," you say, sliding her sleeve up her arm, "is about trust."

You slide two fingers over her wrist, feeling the bone underneath, and rub her skin in circles. "You're not just giving your blood to another. You're *letting them* draw that blood. You're trusting them not to take more than you can give, even if you are willing. You're trusting them not to cut deeper than you can take. You're trusting them to see your bleeding, wounded, ugly self, and stand by you anyway."

You pause your fingers over her pulse, looking back at her face. Her expression surprises you. Her pupils are blown wide. Her lips are parted. For a second, you mistake it for shock, or maybe fascination, but then you pick up the speed of her pulse beneath your fingers, and-

"Simin, are you-"

She takes her arm away so fast you might as well have burned her. "Shut up."

Well, alright then. You close your mouth and looks down instead, between her-

"*Aurum!*" She hisses. Her hand darts out to grab your chin and force your eyes back on her face.

"You told me not to say anything! I figured we were past the point of checking each other out."

She lets go of your chin and throws her hands in the air. "Fine! Yes! This gave me a boner! The last time we touched skin to skin you had my dick in your mouth, so sue me!"

You burst out laughing, and she drags her palms across her face. Embarrassing her is a treat you will never get tired of, it seems.

"You know," you say as you catch your breath, "I could lend you a hand again, if it's that much of a bother to you."

She glares at you. "We're *supposed* to be *working,* you horndog."

"And we'll work much better once you are no longer distracted." You shrug, palms up. "I am merely offering. Whether anything happens or not is all up to you!"

"I *swear* on every deity on this side of the sea, you are the single most annoying man I have ever had the misfortune to come across." But she still sits on the edge of the altar, hands coming to undo her sheath.

Taking the invitation, you lean forward to kiss the side of her jaw. She tilts her head to the side, so you raise a hand to cup her cheek and let your lips trail lower.

"You have a nice neck," you whisper mindlessly. Your other hand sneaks inside her robes to explore her left thigh. You feel the muscles flex under your touch.

Simin exhales sharply, which may be a snort or may be a sigh. "What, you like my pulse? You get off feeling my life throb under your tongue, Aurum?"

"I think you're mixing up my faith and my kinks, Simin." Though now that she spelled it out, that idea *definitely* appeals to you somewhat. Doubly so that framing things this way would be especially scandalous to Simin.

"What even *are* your kinks." She asks, shifting to spread her legs. "You didn't even have the decency to let me return the favor, last time."

"And while I appreciate the sentiment, I never will." You roll your tongue over the junction between her shoulder and neck. "I'm impotent."

Simin goes till under your touch. "Wait, really?"

"Really." You reply simply. It's not something you feel particularly self-conscious about. It *has* caused some trouble with your past lovers, but Simin is no lover of yours. She's your enemy, your rival, your bitchiest coworker. Which means many things, but mostly that you are confident she will not try to *fix* your relationship to pleasure out of some misguided pity.

She laughs briefly. "You know, people like you said to be the ideal priest for Lamuker."

Now *you're* the one to pause. "You're kidding me."

"I'm serious! Something about how people impervious to the pleasures of the flesh can dedicate more of themselves to the goddess, or something."

This makes you laugh as well. Because the reasoning is stupid, because she brings it up *now* of all times, because *Lamuker* of all people would welcome you for this. "Well, *you* wouldn't be an ideal priest to Dum."

You take a second to think. "Though theoretically, you would be a better fit than me, I believe. Our gods have no gender. Genderless people are said to be the most in tune with our gods, but anyone who does not currently live as the gender they were assigned at birth would make a good priest."

Her eyebrows go up in surprise. She does not reply right away; a few seconds pass as neither of you move. The full irony of the situation is not lost to you. You hold nothing but contempt for her god, and she holds nothing but hatred for yours. How strange of a feeling it is, to be beloved by a being whose opinion you could not care less about.

"This is funny," she says, but she is not laughing. Golden cloth still covers her arms. Silver cloth spreads over your back.

Briefly, you think that the two of you aren't all that different.

"Speaking of gods," you reach out to take her in your hand, and she yelps, taken aback, "Now would be a good time to call upon her. She'll have a *much* better look at you here rather than in our temple."

Your free hand goes up to cup her cheek, then gently turn her head towards the serpentine statue. "Come on. Say hi. Won't you let her see you in the throes of pleasure? It's such a lovely sight. Much better than any offering you could ever give her, I am certain."

Simin growls, snapping her head right back towards you. "You *do* have a kink, you bastard. Blasphemy is what gets you off, isn't it?"

You've never sat down and actually thought about it, but now that she mentions it… "Guilty as charged." But she makes it so satisfying!

She huffs, and then- grabs a fistful of your collar. You squeak in surprise, and she laughs in your face.

"Watch out, little man. One day I'll find a way to turn *you* away from your god."

Suddenly, you remember that Simin is 1) much taller than you, and 2) much *stronger* than you, two things that really, *really* get you going.

She drags you into a kiss, all tongue and heat and *hunger.* You respond by jerking her off with renewed vigor, each of her a wordless encouragement. You bite at her lips, she tugs on your collar, you drag your thumb over the head of her cock, and-

She comes in your hand, hot and sticky and *Simin,* and at this moment, you think it feels a lot like blood.

V

"We are *not* doing this here ever again," is the first thing Simin says once she's done catching her breath.

You are wiping your hands with the first cloth you could find. If it was something important, well, then, sucks to be her. "So you are open to doing this *elsewhere* then?"

You hoped to embarrass her, but this only gets her to roll her eyes. Damn it. "One is an accident, two is a pattern. Until we resolve this wedding matter, this is bound to happen again."

"Isn't the saying *one is an accident, two is a coincidence, three is a pattern?*"

"I don't think it works if the second time is a coincidence on purpose."

You raise an eyebrow at that. "*Was* it on purpose? I wasn't aware people could just get it up on command."

She moves to throw something at you, and you quickly dart out of the way; only to realize that she had nothing to throw to begin with. Now you feel a bit stupid. "I meant how *you* keep enticing me anytime I get a boner."

"*Enticing*. It takes two to tango, you know? I vividly remember you giving me your blessing."

"Fine. So we've *both* contributed to make those accident happens, and because we are contrarian little shits as well as good lays, these will probably happen again." She huffs, retying her sash with harsh movements. "Still not doing it on this altar ever again. This one is no-negotiable."

Disheartening, but fair. "Do you guys have a rule about that too? Genuine question. I want to know if your rulebook have prepared for that kind of scenario."

"Not to my knowledge." She answers curtly. "But I think we can agree that most people wouldn't appreciate others fucking on their table, and gods are no exception."

A sound, if odd reasoning. "So it's common to all Khaesans?"

She does not respond immediately, which you take as a *duh*. You think you're starting to understand how their religion works.

"Why Khaesan?"

Mh?

"Khaesan. It means *false god,* does it not?" She's staring at you with a look you cannot decipher. There is no anger or hatred there, or is there confusion or offense. There is only one thing in her voice, and it feels like, it sounds like-

A genuine, profound desire to *understand.*

"I thought you labelled any god foreign to your land as such. That I would understand. But I've heard

Sand People refer to some of our gods plainly as *gods,* with no adjectives. I cannot for the life of me figure out the difference. So why false god? What is the difference?"

It surprises you. That she would be trying so hard to figure it out. That she would *care* so much. You knew she didn't mind the worshipping of gods from your homeland- Dum alone, the blood alone, your offerings alone make her skin crawl- but you'd assumed she simply lived and let live. You thought she was merely hearing; you didn't think she was *listening.*

How can you answer? Because you have to, you have to. She's reaching out, she's asking you; you cannot just slap her hand away. How can you answer? How can you explain something so obvious yet vague, something so fundamental to your culture as a whole? How can anyone answer the question *what is a god?*

"… In the Sand Tongue," you start, "we use the same word to mean *to rule* and *to be.* It is not that we are

50

lacking in vocabulary. But to us, those two concepts are functionally the same thing."

You make a general gesture at your entire being. "I am Aurum. I rule over all that makes me. My choices. My desires. My body. My emotions. I may not control them all, but they are my domain regardless. Because I am Aurum."

Simin's entire attention is on you. She does not snide a snarky comment. She does not roll her eyes, or raise her eyebrows, or interrupt you.

She simply stares. She stares, and she listens.

"It works the other way around, too. To be the king of a country is to *be* that country. It means embodying, its culture, its power, its *will*. The land is to a ruler what a body is to a person."

Something shifts in her features. Finally, she's starting to get it.

"And it's the same for gods."

This, at least, gets her voice to rise: "Ah."

Ah, indeed.

"To us, a god of fire is not a being that controls fire, or a being represented by fire, or anything like this. A god of fire *is* fire, in its every aspects, protective warmth and helpful heat and destructive flames. Asking our gods for their preferences is akin to asking a mountain for a reply. Our gods have no taboos and no rules, because these are human concepts asked from beings who are very much *not* human."

You glance to the right, to Lamuker's statue. "You said it yourself, did you not? *Most people wouldn't appreciate others fucking on their table.* Your gods, khaesans- they're *people.* They have faces, and desires, and opinions. They're people. Powerful people, fearsome people, respectable people. But people nonetheless. The sturdiest person in the world will never be a stone. And your gods, they're certainly divine, in a way, in how they are worshipped, in how they're beloved. But they're not true gods. And they never will be."

There is a moment of silence, following your explanation. You cannot read Simin's face. She could be offended, or enlightened, or even spacing out, you have no way to know. It's completely different from her usual behavior. It is, honestly, a bit jarring.

And then, slowly, she nods.

"The two of us…" her voice is as quiet as the hour before dawn. "We will never see eye to eye, will we?"

You shake your head. "No. I don't believe we will."

This isn't just a matter of differing vocabulary, or conflicting rites, or anything of the sort. Your very conceptions of the world are different. The very way you perceive and interact with what you qualify as divine are direct opposite.

No. The two of you will never stand on the same side.

But she reached out, here. She reached out, and you reached back, and though it did not result in any sort of agreement or understanding, it means something, you think.

VI

Children are not allowed to give offerings to Dum, for obvious reasons; someone's health will always be prioritized over someone's faith. Parents are usually the ones to bleed for their children on the altar, their everyday efforts and sacrifices made literal within the temple.

If that is not possible, for any reason, the priest is the one to give the blood. Oh, the worshipper still has to be the one to hold the knife, but by cutting they establish a link between the priest and themself, and by bleeding the priest establishes a link between them and Dum. This way, anyone, even children, even the elderly, even the sick can honor their faith as they wish.

Your blood is warm against your skin, running in tiny rivulets all the way to the stone table. You still remember the day you got to bleed for yourself for the first time. You remember thinking it was an odd sensation, your life dripping out of open cuts that do not carry any pain. It tingled unlike anything you have ever felt- like a whisper below the skin, like a gentle touch murmured by your ear. It felt holy. And, though you have now long gotten used to it- it still does.

Distantly, you hear the temple door open. It closes slowly and quietly, as if the intruder was afraid to disturb the very air. You have an inkling as to who that may be; you do know of *someone* who is used to gigantic doors that cause a racket if you don't use them carefully.

Footsteps come closer. She does not speak up or interrupt you in any way. Soon, your prayers start to follow the rhythm of her breathing. This goes on for a minute or so, and then you open your eyes.

"Good day to you, Simin." You greet at last, applying the flat of the blade against your wrists. "I did not expect to see you today."

Simin nods to greet you back. Just like last time, her gaze is transfixed by your forearms. Her eyes are dark and filled with thunderclouds. Her displeasure is apparent. "I didn't intend on interrupting you. My apologies."

It might be the first time she has ever apologized to you about anything. Weirdly enough, you don't feel like making fun of her for it. "It's fine." You make a vague gesture of the hand. Your wounds closed, you set down the knife, and reach out for the rag. "What's today's order of business-?"

Fingers close around your wrist.

"… Simin?" You abandon your search of the rag to look at her. She has stepped closer to you while you weren't looking. She's still staring at your forearms, but considering your cuts are healed and you're about to wipe off the blood, you're a bit confused as to what could be the issue. "Simin, you'll get blood on you."

She does not answer. She raises your hand, higher than your hip, higher than your chest, higher than your head, and she brings it closer to her, and then she

Licks

It.

For a second, you forget to breathe.

Her tongue swirls over your wrist, where the wound use to be, warmth and wetness mixing with the remnant of the divine tingle. The sensation makes your head spin. She holds your hand in place the way one would hold a knife; firmly, purposely, and with indescribable affection.

"…Simin?"

She looks up at you, pupils blown wide with emotions you cannot read. Her lips are smudged red in the most macabre of make-up.

"You look," her voice has always been on the deep side; right now, it's like an echo, like a purr, like the depths of the nights calling *join us, join us, come in and walk and walk and walk where no one will ever find you again,* "really good covered in blood."

It was on purpose, you realize. If she aimed for your wrist and nowhere else. If she stained her lips red. If she's looking at you with those wide eyes and bared teeth and-

It's not disgust. It was never disgust.

It's *arousal.*

"It was the blood," you let out, the realization washing over you like tides on the shore, "that first time. You also came in while I was praying back then. You didn't just pop a boner out of nowhere. It was the *blood.*"

Her mouth parts from your skin, and you watch her licking her lips. "Congratulations, Aurum. Your endeavors to corrupt me are a success."

Oh, this- this is rich. This is hilarious. This is elating. This is shivers down your spine and clouds in

your lungs and fire on your tongue and a thousand other things and every single one of them chants *yes, yes, yes.*

Is this what it means to be seduced? You feel very seduced at this moment.

You present her your other wrist, and she latches onto it like a feral thing. You remember the red on her hands that other time, those paintings she refuses to show anyone. Does she look like this, when she paints? Has anyone else gotten to see her like this- bloody, unhinged, at her rawest and most base self?

The two of you, you're two sides of the same coin. Opposite, never to reach an agreement- but no one has ever understood her the way you have. No one will ever understand you the way she does.

She leaves your wrist with a last kiss, your arm now clean if sticky with spit. She reaches out to the side. You watch her take hold of the silver knife, and you do not move. She could dig it inside your guts right now and you still wouldn't move.

But she doesn't. She hands it to you instead, and she says, in a husky voice: "I want you."

She does not elaborate, and neither does she need to; you know exactly what she's asking of you, *pleading* of you. Never before have you heard her so vulnerable, so genuine, not even in your most heated arguments, not even during your most debauched sex.

You take the blade. You have only ever used it to pray. As a priest, you have often bled for followers who could not, but whether the cut was for you or for another, the blood was still intended for the same destination- your god. It is, after all, the most intimate of gifts- who else could be worthy of a part of you?

"Congratulations, Simin," you say, echoing her earlier words, "you've managed to corrupt me too."

Then you raise the knife, pull at your collar, and cut into your shoulder.

It's a shallow cut. Skin-deep, really. Just enough for a few beads of blood to bubble up.

This is the most intimate thing you have ever done. Simin presses her entire body against yours, lapping at the wound, and at this moment you think your sacrifice might be enough to turn her into something holy.

(*Sacer facere, sacer facere.*)

You feel her cock against your thighs, hot and hard. You reach down to cup it- but she bats your hand away.

"Keep your wrists where I can see them." She growls, peeling herself away from your skin just to bare her teeth at you.

It's a sight to behold. You've seen Simin angry, horny, in the thrall of desire and the throes of pleasure, but this is the first time you've truly seen her *hungry.* And oh, she is *starving,* this woman, this animal, this god, she's been living with a hole between her ribs for *years* and you are the only one who has the only one who *can* at long last feed her.

You nudge her a bit, just to see if you can, just to see what she'll do- and with a frustrated grunt, she parts from you. She glares at you with all her might, clearly displeased. "Do you want to stop?"

And here it is, what you wanted to test. You may be the one bleeding, but *she* is the one at your mercy. You may be the one bleeding, but you are also the one who wields the knife- the one who decides where and when the wound opens, where and when she gets to taste the red off your brown skin.

She cannot devour you without your consent. And now that you're sure of that, you can give it to her wholeheartedly.

"No. Give me a minute." You reply. You close the wound on your shoulder with the enchanted blade. Then you pause, considering where to cut next.

"I kept the robe, you know. The one you bled on."

You pause, hand trembling, your heart threatening to burst out of your chest. "What?"

"The robe I was wearing when you blew me on your god's altar." She tilts her head towards the stone table for emphasis, though her gaze does not leave you. "The one that dipped in your blood. I still have it. It's still stained by it."

Dizziness overcomes you. You feel warm all over. Burning. Melting. "You did not even wash it, did you?"

She shakes her head, and your soul *sings*.

There are no words, in your tongue or hers, able to express the depths of your feelings. That are no words, in any language, to describe what this means to you. What do you call someone who would kneel to drink your blood out of your cupped hands? What do you call someone you would bare your throat to if asked? What do you call someone who would look at your bare guts and think you beautiful?

Two halves of the same coin, you said earlier, without realizing how right you were. She's your lover, your rival, your enemy, your other half- two people who could never be more different, two people who are never more complete than when they are together. Perhaps this is what it means, to be soulmates. To be tied together down to the soul. To have blood flow through your joined veins.

"That's gross," you tell her, because it kind of is, and because you don't want (you don't know how) to tell her about your epiphany.

She says *"you're* gross," without an hint of offense, and you know that she gets it, too.

"Throw it away." You ready the knife. "I'll give you fresher blood from now on."

The blade digs into your upper arm, drawing a rivulet of red, and Simin's pupils *dilate*.

It all comes down to blood in the end. What she is to you. What you are to her. Whether it's forbidden or required, it's obsession all the same. It all comes down to blood.

The blood is compulsory.

VII

The thought hits you like a bolt of lightning, and you suddenly sit up on the altar still sweating. "The wedding!"

Simin rolls to her side to face you. She's frowning, though the afterglow is massively weakening her glare. "Really? You're gonna bring it up right *now*?"

You ignore her half-hearted jab. She'll survive. "So, hear me out. Lamuker forbids the shedding of blood, right?"

"Yes. We've been over this." She rolls back on her back, crossing her arms over her stomach.

"But *drinking* blood is allowed. Right?"

"It's not exactly *celebrated,* but it is not a direct taboo, yes."

"So, if the girls do what we just did- my follower cutting her wrists and yours drinking some- this wouldn't go against your goddess, would it?"

"I assume this doesn't include them fucking on the altar?" Simin pauses for a few seconds, thinking. "No. It… would work. On my side, at least. Would that be enough for yours?"

You nod. "Definitely. The point of the blood is the intimacy- I would bleed for you, you would bleed for me, I would let you cut me, you would let me cut you. This is close enough to work."

A second of silence pass. Yes. Yes, you think this is a good compromise for the conundrum that has plagued you the entire time.

Just as you think that, however, Simin reaches out to pull on your arm.

"Aurum," she says very seriously, "did *we* just get married."

"What? No! Of course not!" You turn your thoughts back to what you just did. "Probably not. Maybe?" Okay. So. Jot that down as *possibly.* "Would it even work if we didn't get your goddess's blessing?"

"It wouldn't." She says without confidence. "Would it? Fuck, I don't know... Can we be half married? Is that a thing?"

"So, what, I'm married to you, but you're not married to me? Is that it?" You snort. "Did we just invent the first unrequited marriage in history?"

She slaps the back of her hand against your arm. "Of course not, don't be stupid. History is so weird, we can't possibly be the *first* ones."

You burst out laughing, pure joy flaring from your lungs. Who'd have thought Simin could be funny when she's not busy biting your nose off? Just a couple months ago, the idea wouldn't even have occurred to you.

"Let's be serious for a second, though," you manage between two wheezes, "do you *want* to get married?"

"To *you?*" And now *she's* the one snorting. "Aurum, we'd kill each other within a week."

"Oh, ye of little faith." You shake your head. "I bet we could manage a month."

"Ah, I feel so much better now. Certainly, murder's a less grievous charge past the first week living together."

"Obviously. Do you know nothing of law?" You chuckle. "Besides, I'd let you do it."

"Murder you?"

"Sure." You set two fingers right under your jaw, at the beginning of the throat. Then, slowly, you drag them down to your collarbone. Her eyes follow the movement. "I'd show you where to cut. How to make it real bloody. You can only kill me once, best to make it as good as possible, don't you agree?"

A pause. "You are," Simin closes her eyes, "*insanely* fucking weird."

"As opposed to you, who spent the last half hour sucking my blood." You flick her arm. "Admit it. You would do the same."

"... Unfortunately, yes." She sighs. "I'd show you where to light the fire. I'd sit down and watch the flames dance, and know this is your last performance to me."

What a pair the two of you make. Bearers of compatible insanity.

"Ask me about the marriage again in a few years." Simin says suddenly, and you blink.

"Come again?"

"I said, ask me about the marriage again in a few years." She repeats herself. "You are... more bearable than I expected. I want to see where it goes... whatever this is."

"… Well, I will certainly do." It's not conventional- not for her people and not for yours- but you *are* curious, and… you do want to keep what the two of you have. Strange as that relationship may be.

You lean down, and you kiss her, and on her lips you taste your own blood.

* 9 7 9 8 2 0 1 0 0 5 6 4 1 *